D1355252

LINGTON LIBRARIES

3 0120 02033896 8

N4 Library
26 Blackstock Road
London N4 2DW
Tel: 020 7527 7800

GTON

THIS BOOK BELONGS TO:

Other Kipper books

Kipper
Kipper's Toybox
Kipper's Birthday
Kipper's Snowy Day
Kipper's Christmas Eve
Where, Oh Where, is Kipper's Bear?
Kipper's Book of Colours
Kipper's Book of Opposites
Kipper's Book of Counting
Kipper's Book of Weather
The Little Kippers
Kipper Story Collection
Kipper's A to Z

Skates

Mick Inkpen

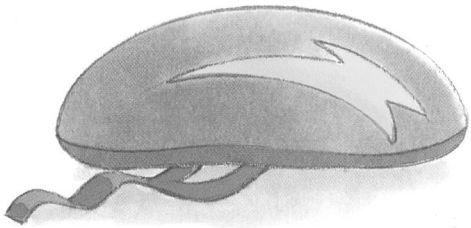

ISLINGTON LIBRARIES	
30120020338968	
PETERS	13-Nov-06
£3.99	
F	

Hodder Children's Books

A division of Hodder Headline Limited

Tiger had some brand new skates.

'They're called Roller Blades,' said Tiger. 'Much better than ordinary skates, Kipper. Look, the wheels are all in a line!'

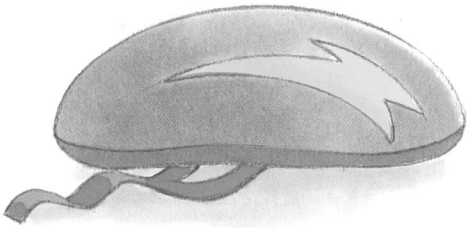

Tiger was not very good on his new skates. He kept wobbling and falling on his bottom.

Then he rolled off down the path, waving his arms and shouting, 'Get out of the way!'

He crashed into Pig, who was walking Arnold in the park.

Tiger struggled to his feet, and then fell over again.

'I haven't got any skates,' said Pig. 'Can I have a go?'

'No,' said Tiger.

'No, I wouldn't want you to hurt yourself. No.'

So Kipper let Pig have a go of his skates instead.

Pig was a terrible skater. He couldn't even stand up!

'What you need is practice,' said Tiger. He was so busy telling Pig how to do it, that he didn't notice himself rolling down the slope again.

He crashed into a bush.

'Ow!' shouted Tiger.
He had hurt his thumb.
'Ow! Ow! Ow!' He wasn't
very brave.

Kipper took him home for
a sticking plaster. Tiger wanted
some ointment, a bandage,
a sling and a sweetie too!

'Let's go and show Pig my
bandage!' he said.

When they arrived at Pig's house, Pig and Arnold were in the garden. Pig was still wearing Kipper's skates.

'I want to show you something!' said Pig. He put on some music and began to skate.

'Wow!' said Kipper and Tiger together.
Pig had been practising.
He was brilliant!

And Arnold wasn't bad, either.

First published 2001
by Hodder Children's Books,
a division of Hodder Headline Limited,
338 Euston Road, London NW1 3BH

Copyright © Mick Inkpen 1998

10 9 8 7 6 5 4 3 2 1

ISBN 0 340 81814 X

A catalogue record for this book
is available from the British Library.

The right of Mick Inkpen to be identitfied
as the author of this Work
has been asserted by him in accordance with
the copyrights, Designs and Patents Act 1988.

All rights reserved

Printed in Hong Kong